First Fairy Tales

For Roderick, Katrina
and Andrew

ORCHARD BOOKS
338 Euston Road, London NW1 3BH
Orchard Books Australia
Level 17/207 Kent Street, Sydney, NSW 2000
First published in Great Britain in 1994 by Orchard Books
This edition published in 2004
ISBN 978 1 84362 400 4
Text © Margaret Mayo 1994
Illustrations © Selina Young 1994
The rights of Margaret Mayo to be identified as the author
and Selina Young to be identified as the illustrator
of this work has been asserted by them in accordance
with the Copyright, Designs and Patents Act, 1988.
A CIP catalogue record for this book is available from the British Library.
3 5 7 9 10 8 6 4 2
Printed in Singapore
Orchard Books is a division of Hachette Children's Books,
an Hachette Livre UK company.
www.hachettelivre.co.uk

First Fairy Tales

Retold by Margaret Mayo
Illustrated by Selina Young

ORCHARD BOOKS

Jack and the Beanstalk

Once upon a time, there was a boy called Jack, and he lived with his mother in a little house in the country. They were poor and didn't have much of anything. But they did have a cow. Her name was Milky-White.

One day, when there was no money left to buy any food, Jack's mother told him to take Milky-

White to market and sell her. So off he went with the cow.

On the way, Jack saw an old man walking down the road, holding his hat very carefully in both hands.

"Hello!" said the old man. "And where are you going this sunshiny day?"

"I'm going to market to sell our cow."

"That's where I'm going," said the old man. "I want to sell these five beans I've got in my hat.

They are MAGIC BEANS! If you plant them, they'll grow to the sky and then you can climb up and get all the treasure that's up there!"

"Oh, I'd like to do that!" said Jack.

"Well," said the old man, "let's swop your cow for my beans!"

"All right," said Jack. And he gave the cow to

the old man, took the beans, put them in his pocket and ran home.

When he saw his mother, Jack said, "Look what I got for the cow – FIVE MAGIC BEANS! If you plant them … "

"What!" said his mother. "You didn't sell our cow for five beans? Oh, Jack! How could you do such a thing?"

She was really cross. She grabbed the beans and flung them out of the window. Then she sent Jack up to his room, straight to bed.

In the morning, the first thing Jack saw was a whole lot of big dangly leaves outside his window. He jumped out of bed and threw on his clothes, any old how,

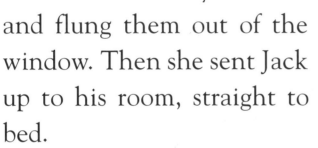

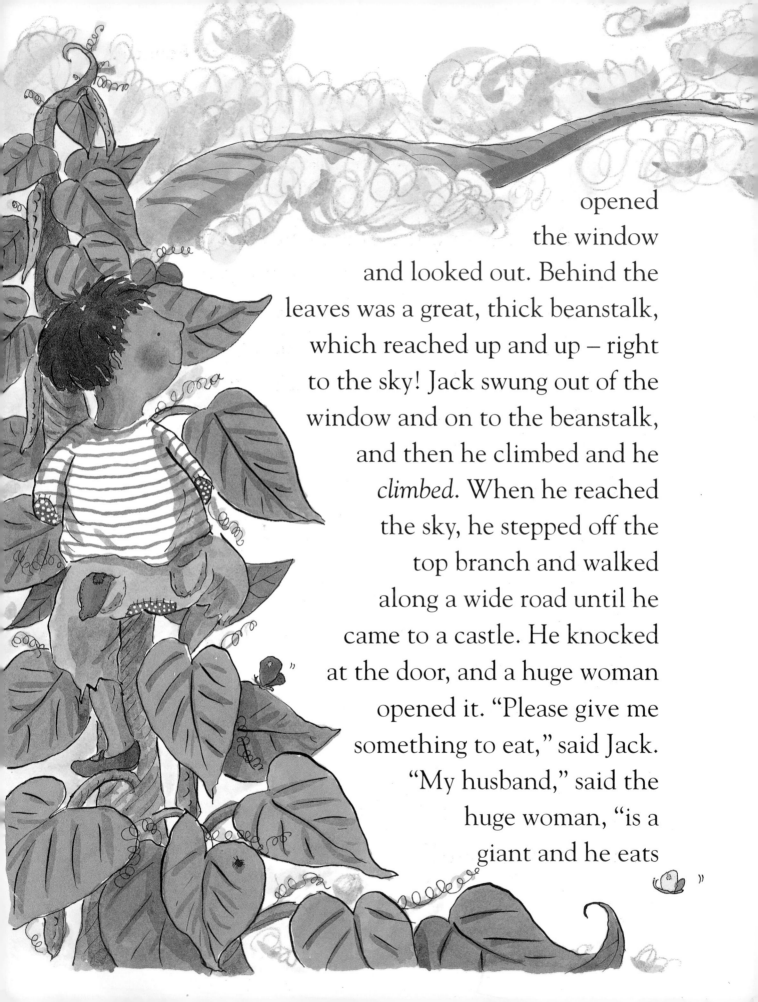

opened the window and looked out. Behind the leaves was a great, thick beanstalk, which reached up and up – right to the sky! Jack swung out of the window and on to the beanstalk, and then he climbed and he *climbed*. When he reached the sky, he stepped off the top branch and walked along a wide road until he came to a castle. He knocked at the door, and a huge woman opened it. "Please give me something to eat," said Jack. "My husband," said the huge woman, "is a giant and he eats little boys for breakfast. So, run away before he comes home and catches you!"

"But I'm hungry," said Jack.

Well, in the end the giant's wife asked him in and gave him a hunk of bread, a lump of cheese and a mug of milk. But before Jack had finished eating, there was a *thump! thump! thump!*

"Quick – hide!" said the giant's wife and she pushed Jack into the oven. In stamped the giant, roaring: *"Fee fi fo fum! I smell the blood of an English man!"*

"No, dear," said his wife. "It's the twenty juicy chops, freshly fried for your breakfast. That's what you smell!"

And with that she went off to do some housework, while the giant ate his breakfast. When he had finished, he stamped over to a big chest, took out his money-bag and counted his gold. Then he closed his eyes and began to snore.

So – Jack crept out of the oven, picked up the money-bag and tiptoed out. He ran along the road

and climbed down the beanstalk.

When his mother saw the gold, she was pleased. Now they could buy as much food as they wanted and smart new clothes besides.

BUT … after a while, Jack began to wonder what other treasures there were up in the sky, and early one morning he climbed the beanstalk again. He walked along the wide road, and when he came to the castle, he knocked at the door and asked the giant's wife for something to eat.

She said, "Are you the rascally boy who came here the day my husband lost his money-bag?"

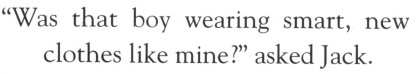

"Was that boy wearing smart, new clothes like mine?" asked Jack.

"No-o," she said. "No-o, he wasn't. Must have been someone else."

Once again, she invited Jack in and gave him a hunk of bread, a lump of cheese and a mug of milk. And when she heard the giant coming, she hid Jack in the oven.

In stamped the giant, roaring: "*Fee fi fo fum! I smell the blood of an English man!*"

"No, dear," said his wife. "It's the twenty juicy sausages, freshly fried for your breakfast. That's what you smell!"

And with that she went off to do some housework, while the giant ate his breakfast. When he had finished, he stamped over to a cage, took out a hen, put her on the table and said, "Lay!" And the hen laid a *golden* egg. Then he closed his eyes and began to snore.

So – Jack crept out of the oven, picked up the hen and tiptoed out. He ran along the road and climbed down the beanstalk.

He ran into the house, put the hen on the kitchen table and said, "Lay!" And the hen laid a *golden* egg. Again he said, "Lay!" And the hen laid *another*

golden egg. When his mother saw the golden eggs, she was very pleased. Now they could have gold any time they wanted. They were rich.

BUT … after a while, Jack began to wonder what other treasures there were up in the sky, and early one morning he climbed the beanstalk again. This time he didn't knock at the castle door. He hid behind a bush, and when the giant's wife came out to peg her washing on the line, Jack hurried inside.

Now where could he hide? He saw a large bin with BREAD written on it, so he climbed in and pulled the lid on top. Then the giant's wife came back, and in stamped the giant, roaring: "*Fee fi fo fum! I smell the blood of an English man!*"

"Look in the oven," said his wife. "If that rascally boy who took your money-bag and your hen has come back, that's where he will be!"

The giant looked in the oven. But it was empty!

Then the giant's wife went off to do some housework, while the giant ate his breakfast. When he had finished, he stamped over to a cupboard, took out a golden harp and said, "Sing!" And the harp

17

played sweet music. Then the giant closed his eyes and began to snore.

So – Jack crept out of the bread bin and picked up the golden harp. But the harp sang out, "Master! Master!" Then Jack ran - fast as he could!

The giant woke, and when he saw Jack running off with the harp, he roared, "I will catch you, rascally boy!"

Jack ran along the wide road, and the giant ran after him. Jack reached the beanstalk and began to climb down ... down ... down.

The giant reached the beanstalk and he began to climb down. And that giant came closer ... and closer … and closer.

When Jack was nearly at the bottom, he shouted, "Mother! Quick, bring an axe!"

And his mother came running out of the house with an axe. Jack jumped to the ground and put down the harp. He picked up the axe and chopped through the beanstalk – and the beanstalk came tumbling down and the giant with it. And that giant fell so hard and so fast, it was the end of him!

From then on, Jack and his mother had everything they needed. If they wanted money, they said, "Lay!"

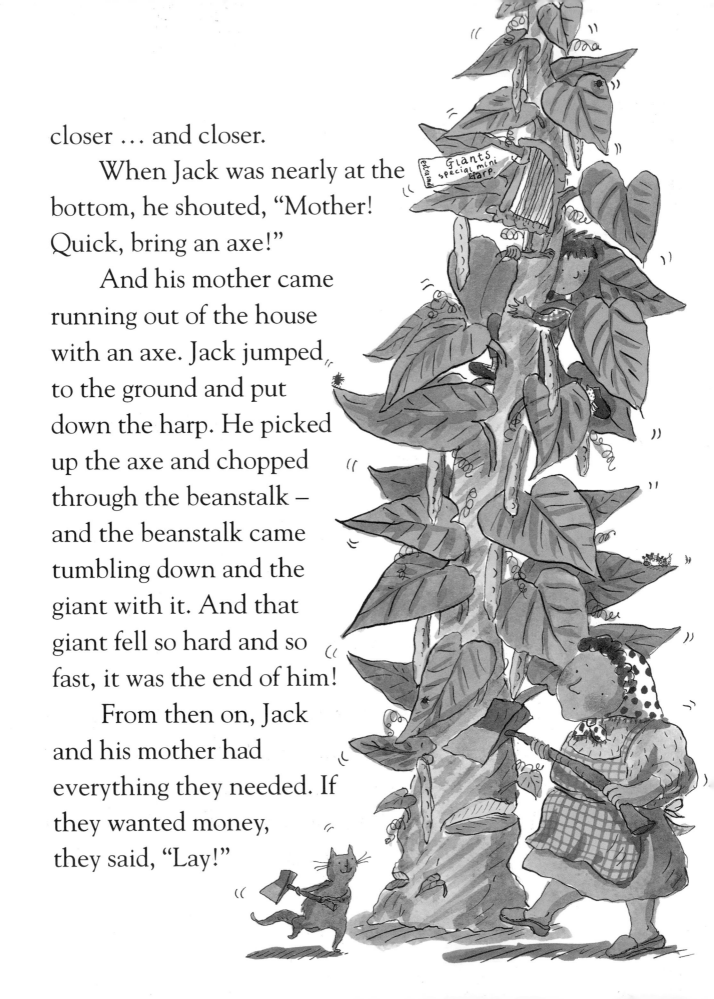

and the wonderful hen gave them a golden egg. If they were tired or sad, they said, "Sing!" and the golden harp played sweet music. And they had all this because Jack swopped their cow, Milky-White, for FIVE MAGIC BEANS!

Cinderella

Once upon a time, there was a beautiful girl called Cinderella, and she had two ugly stepsisters who were very unkind and made her do all the hard work. She had to sweep the floors, cook the food and wash the dirty dishes, while they dressed up in fine clothes and went to lots of parties.

One day a special invitation arrived at

21

royal invitation

Cinderella's house. It was from the royal palace. The king's only son, who was a truly handsome prince, was going to have a grand ball, and the three girls were invited to come!

Cinderella knew she wouldn't be allowed to go to the ball. But the ugly sisters ... oh! they were excited. They couldn't talk about anything else.

When the day of the ball came, they made such a fuss. Poor Cinderella had to rush about, upstairs and downstairs. She fixed their hair in

fancy waves and curls. She helped them put on their expensive new dresses. And she arranged their jewels, just so!

As soon as they had gone, Cinderella sat down by the fire, and she said, "I do wish I could go to the ball!"

The next moment, standing beside her was a lovely old lady with a silver wand in her hand.

"Cinderella," she said, "I am your fairy godmother, and you *shall* go to the ball! But, first, you must go into the garden and pick a golden pumpkin. Then bring me six mice from the mouse-traps, a whiskery rat from the rat-trap and

six lizards. You'll find the lizards behind the watering can."

So Cinderella fetched a golden pumpkin, six grey mice, a whiskery rat and six lizards.

The fairy godmother touched them with her wand … and the pumpkin became a golden coach, the mice became six grey horses, the rat became a coachman with the most enormous moustache and the lizards became six footmen dressed in green and yellow.

Then the fairy godmother touched Cinderella with the wand … and her old dress became a golden dress sparkling with jewels, while on her feet was the prettiest pair of glass slippers ever seen.

"Remember," said the fairy godmother, "you must leave the ball before the clock strikes twelve, because at midnight the magic ends."

"Thank you, kind fairy godmother," said Cinderella. And she climbed into the coach.

When Cinderella arrived at the ball, she looked so beautiful that everyone wondered who she was. Even the ugly sisters! The prince, of course, asked her to dance with him, and they danced all evening. He would not dance with anyone else.

Now Cinderella was enjoying the ball so much that she forgot her fairy godmother's warning, until it was almost midnight and the clock began to strike.

One ... two ... three ... she hurried out of the ballroom. *Four ... five ... six ...* as she ran down the palace steps, one of her glass slippers fell off. *Seven ... eight ... nine ...* she ran on towards the golden coach. *Ten ... eleven ... TWELVE!*

Then ... there was Cinderella in her old dress. A golden pumpkin lay at her feet, and scampering off down the road were six grey mice, a whiskery

rat and six green lizards. So Cinderella had to walk home, and by the time the ugly sisters returned, she was sitting quietly by the fire.

Now when Cinderella ran from the palace, the prince tried to follow her, and he found the glass slipper.

He said, "I shall marry the beautiful girl whose foot fits this slipper – and only her!"

In the morning the prince went from house to house with the glass slipper, and every young lady tried to squeeze her foot into it. But it didn't fit any of them.

At last the prince came to Cinderella's house. First one ugly sister tried to squash her foot into the slipper, but her foot was too wide and fat. Then the other ugly sister tried, but her foot was too long and thin.

"Please," said Cinderella, "let me try."

"The slipper won't fit you!" said the ugly sisters. "You didn't go to the ball!"

But Cinderella slipped her foot into the glass slipper, and it fitted perfectly. The next moment, standing beside her was the fairy godmother. She touched Cinderella with the wand … and there she was in a golden dress sparkling with jewels, and on her feet was the prettiest pair of glass slippers ever seen.

The ugly sisters were so surprised that, for once, they couldn't think of anything to say! But the prince knew what to say – he asked Cinderella to marry him.

And then there was a happy wedding. Everyone who had gone to the ball was invited – even the ugly sisters! There was wonderful food and lots of music and dancing. And the prince, of course, danced every dance with Cinderella. He would not dance with anyone else!

Puss in Boots

Once upon a time, in a windmill on top of a hill, there lived an old man and his three sons. When the old man died, he left the windmill to the eldest son, a donkey to the second and a cat called Puss to the third.

The youngest son was upset. He wanted to have the windmill or the donkey. "I am fond of you, Puss," he said, as he stroked the cat, "but

you're not very useful. Except for catching mice!"

Puss looked up. "Not very useful?" he said. "Get me a bag and a pair of soft leather boots, and I'll show you what I can do!"

So the lad found a bag, and then he fetched his best, soft leather boots. Puss pulled on the boots, and they s-h-r-a-n-k until they fitted perfectly. Then he rose up on his hind legs, slung the bag over his shoulder and marched off down the road.

When he came to a field where there were lots of rabbit holes, he picked some dandelion leaves, stuffed them in the bag and made a rabbit trap. Before long, a plump rabbit poked its head out of a hole, hopped into the bag and began to eat the leaves. Then that clever Puss slung the bag over his shoulder, marched off to the king's palace and gave the rabbit to the king.

"Your Majesty," said Puss, bowing very low, "here is a present from my master, the Duke of Carabas."

And the king said, "I thank your master, the Duke of Carabas."

Then off went Puss, with the empty bag over his shoulder.

Next morning, he marched down the road again. When he came to a cornfield where there were lots of partridges, he picked some corn, dropped it in the bag and made a partridge trap. And that clever Puss caught two plump partridges and took them to the king.

The next morning Puss said to the lad, "Today you must come with me and do exactly what I

tell you!"

So they marched off, side by side, until they came to a river that flowed past the king's palace.

"Every afternoon," said Puss, "the king goes for a drive in the country with his daughter, who is the most beautiful princess in the world. Today you shall meet this princess – and then you shall marry her. But first, take off your shabby old clothes and jump in the river!"

So the lad took off his clothes, jumped in the river and swam around, while Puss picked everything up, stuffed it in his bag and hid the bag under a large stone.

Before long, the royal coach came bowling down the road. "Help! Help!" shouted Puss, waving a paw.

When the king saw the wonderful cat who had brought him such lovely presents, he stopped the coach and called out, "What is the matter?"

"Your Majesty," said Puss, "while my master the Duke of Carabas was swimming, some robbers came and stole his clothes, and now he has nothing to wear."

"Nothing to wear?" said the king. "That won't do!" And he ordered one of his guards to go and fetch some splendid new clothes from the palace.

When the guard came back with the clothes, the lad climbed out of the river and put them on. And then he looked so handsome and grand – just like a real duke!

He bowed to the king and the beautiful princess and he said, "Your Majesty, I thank you for your kindness."

"And I thank you, Duke of Carabas, for the presents you sent me," said the king. "Now, will you join the princess and myself on our ride through the country?"

So the lad climbed into the coach, and they were off.

And Puss – what about him? He ran ahead until he came to an enormous cornfield where some men were busy cutting the corn. Puss marched up to them and said, "Listen! When the king comes by, you must tell him that this field and the land round about belong to the Duke of Carabas. If you don't, I shall chop you into mince meat!"

When the royal coach came bowling along and the king saw the enormous cornfield, he called out, "Who owns this field?"

And the men sang out, "This field and the land round about belong to the Duke of Carabas!"

The king thought, "*Hmmm...* This duke must be rich!"

And Puss – what about him? He ran on until he came to a huge castle which belonged to a fierce ogre. He marched up to the door, took hold of the knocker and banged it down. *Bam! bam! bam!*

A window opened. The ogre stuck out his head and shouted, "WHO'S THERE?"

"A stranger," answered Puss. "One who has heard of your mighty powers and wants to meet you."

The ogre came clumping down the stairs and opened the door. Puss stepped in and followed him into the great hall.

"I have heard," said Puss, "that you can change yourself into any sort of animal ... an elephant ... a lion ... anything!"

"True!" said the ogre.

And ... *vrooom*! he was a lion.

Puss was so scared he jumped on to the mantelpiece and hung on tight – and that was not easy with those boots on his feet!

Then ... *vrooom*! the lion was an ogre again.

"Amazing!" said Puss. "You scared me then – just a little!" And he jumped down from the mantelpiece. "I have also heard," he went on, "that you can change into a tiny animal, like a mouse. But that must be impossible for a huge ogre like you!"

"IMPOSSIBLE?" shouted the ogre. He was angry. "What do you mean, IMPOSSIBLE?"

And ... *vrooom!* he was a mouse running across the floor.

Puss was quick. One big leap and he caught the mouse ... and he gobbled it up!

A few moments later, Puss heard the sound of coach wheels and the clippetty-clop of horses' hooves, so he marched outside. He bowed and said, "Welcome to the castle of my master, the Duke of Carabas!"

The king looked up at the huge castle and he thought, "*Hmmm* ... this duke must be *very* rich!"

Then Puss led them all into the great hall. It was crammed full of wonderful things and the king thought, "*Hmmm* ... this duke must be *very, very* rich!"

He said, "Duke of Carabas, if you want to marry my daughter, you only have to ask!"

The lad looked at the beautiful princess, and she looked at him; and they both smiled. So he asked her to marry him. After that, there was a wedding!

And clever Puss – what about him? He lived for many happy years in the ogre's castle with his master and the beautiful princess. They both made a great fuss of him. He had his own velvet cushion by the fire, plenty of saucers full of cream and lots of other tasty treats!

The Sleeping Beauty

Once upon a time, there was a king and queen, and when their baby daughter was born, they were so happy, they decided to have a big party. They invited all their family, all their friends *and* all the fairies in the land.

Now there were thirteen fairies altogether, but the king and queen only invited twelve. They forgot about the thirteenth ... and that was something they should not have done!

Well, it was a splendid party. There were silver dishes piled high with delicious food and golden plates in every place. And when everyone had finished eating, the fairies gathered around the baby's cradle, and they each made a magic wish.

"The princess shall be beautiful," said the first.

"And happy," said the second.

"And kind," said the third.

And so they went on. The princess was to be brave and clever and truthful. She was to have a sweet singing voice and light dancing feet. And then … just as the twelfth fairy was about to make her wish, in came the thirteenth! She was furious

because she had not been invited to the party.

"Here is my wish," she said. "When the princess is sixteen years old, she will prick her finger on a spindle and she will die!" And with that, the thirteenth fairy vanished.

Then the twelfth fairy said, "I cannot change all of the wicked fairy's powerful magic. So the princess *will* prick her finger, but she will not die. She will fall asleep for a hundred years."

The king and queen thanked the twelfth fairy for her kindness, but they were not happy. They did not want their daughter to sleep for a hundred years, so they ordered that every spindle and spinning-wheel in the land must be chopped up

and burnt. Then they thought that the princess was safe.

The years passed, and the princess grew up. She was very beautiful and clever at lots of different things. She was, in fact, everything the fairies had wished her to be.

On her sixteenth birthday, the princess was exploring the castle, when she came to a little room at the top of a tall tower … and in that room was an old woman, sitting by a spinning-wheel.

"What are you doing?" asked the princess.

"I am spinning," said the old woman – who was really the wicked thirteenth fairy. "Would you like to try?"

"Oh, yes!" said the princess. And she sat down by the spinning-wheel.

But as soon as she touched the spindle, the sharp point pricked her finger … and she fell asleep … and the old woman vanished.

At the same moment the king and queen, the servants, the cats and the dogs all fell asleep. Even the fire stopped burning and the roasting meat stopped sizzling. Everything slept. Then a hedge of wild roses grew up around the castle. It grew and it grew, until the castle was hidden.

One hundred years passed, and then a prince came riding by and saw the top of a tower rising up above the hedge of roses.

"How strange," he said. "I never knew there was a castle here."

He jumped off his horse and lifted his sword to cut a way through the hedge. But as soon as the sword touched a branch, a path opened up in front of him. So the prince walked freely through the hedge.

He entered the castle and walked from room to room. Imagine his surprise! Everyone and everything was fast asleep! At last he entered a little room at the top of a tall tower, and he saw the sleeping princess. She was so very beautiful that he bent down and kissed her.

Then the spell was broken, and the princess opened her eyes. At the same moment, everybody and everything in the castle awoke. The king yawned, the queen blinked, the cats had a good stretch and the dogs wagged their tails. The servants began to work, the fire began to flame and the roasting meat began to sizzle. A hundred years had not changed anyone or anything.

And what happened next? Why, the beautiful princess married the prince who had woken her from such a long, deep sleep.

Rumpelstiltskin

Once upon a time there was a foolish farmer who was always showing off and this farmer had a clever beautiful daughter.

One day the farmer went to the palace and started to do some showing off. He said to the king, "I have a very beautiful daughter!"

But the king took no notice. So the farmer said, "And she's clever too! She is so clever, she can … SPIN STRAW INTO GOLD!"

The king's eyes almost popped out of his head. He loved gold. "Oh-ho!" he said. "I'd like to see this daughter of yours!"

Then the farmer hurried home and told his daughter that she must go to the palace, because the king wanted to see for himself how clever and beautiful she was.

But when the girl, all happy and proud, got to the palace, the king took her to a room where there was a pile of straw and a spinning-wheel.

He said, "Spin this straw into gold!" And off he went.

The girl didn't know what to do, and she

began to cry … and then, in through the window, with a jump and a skip, came a strange little man.

"Beautiful girl," he said, "why are you crying?"

"I must spin this straw into gold," she answered. "And I don't know how to do it."

"What will you give me," said the little man, "if I do it for you?"

"You can have my necklace," she said. And she gave it to him.

The little man sat down. The spinning-wheel whirled round and round, and the straw was spun into gold. Then, with a skip and a jump, he was gone.

In the morning, when the king came and saw the gold, he was pleased. But he wanted *more* gold. So he took the girl to a bigger room, where there was a bigger pile of straw.

He said, "Spin this straw into gold!" And off he went.

Again the girl began to cry … and then, in

through the window, with a jump and a skip, came the strange little man.

"More straw!" he said. "Now what will you give me if I spin it for you?"

"You can have my ring," she said. And she gave it to him.

Again the spinning-wheel whirled round and round, and the straw was spun into gold. Then, with a skip and a jump, the little man was gone.

In the morning, when the king saw the gold, he was very pleased. But he wanted *even more*

gold. So he took the girl to an even bigger room, where there was an even bigger pile of straw. It reached right to the ceiling!

He said, "Spin this straw into gold!" And off he went.

Once again the girl began to cry … and then, in through the window, with a jump and a skip, came the strange little man.

"Even more straw!" he said. "Now what will you give me if I spin it for you?"

"I have nothing left to give," said the girl.

"Then you must promise," he said, "that when you are queen, you will give me your first little baby."

PLEASE FILL
(as full as you
can) from the
KING

"Oh!" she said. "All right … I promise."

Once again the spinning-wheel whirled round and round, and the straw was spun into gold. A huge glittering heap of gold! Then, with a skip and a jump, the little man was gone.

In the morning, when the king saw the gold, he was very, very pleased. Now he had plenty of gold. He thought, "This girl is very clever and she is beautiful too!" So he asked her to marry him— and then the farmer's clever, beautiful daughter became the queen.

A year passed by, and the queen had a baby. She was happy. She had forgotten her promise to the little man. But the little man had not forgotten, and one day when the queen was playing with her baby, he came in through the window.

"Now you must give me your baby," he said.

"Oh, no!" she said. "I'll give you something else. A castle, some jewels. Anything, but not my baby."

"The baby is what I want," he said.

The queen began to cry and cry, and the little man was sorry for her. He said, "If you can guess my name, then you can keep your baby. I will give you three days and three guesses each day."

As soon as the little man had gone, the queen sent servants all over the land to collect lots and lots of different names. And when he came the next day, she tried some unusual ones.

She said, "Is your name Caspar? Is it Jehoshaphat? Is it Balthazar?"

But to each one, he said, "No! That's not my name!"

On the second day, when the little man came, the queen tried some funny names. She said, "Is your name Skinny-legs? Is it Rumble-tummy? Is it Beaky-nose?"

But to each one he said, "No! That's not my name!"

On the morning of the third and last day, the queen thought and she thought, but she couldn't decide which names to try. And then one of the servants hurried in and told her that late at night, when he was walking through the forest, he had seen a strange little man skipping round a fire,

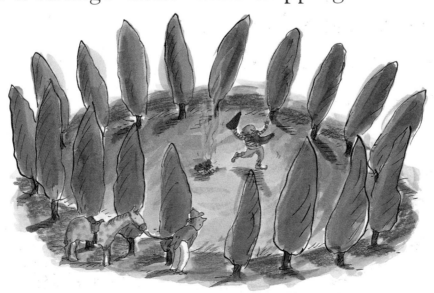

singing this song:

"*Around and around, I dance and I sing,*
And nobody knows I'm Rumpelstiltskin!"

The queen clapped her hands. "That's his name!" she cried. "Rumpelstiltskin!"

When the little man came for the third and last time, he said, "Three guesses-then the baby is mine!"

"I wonder ..." said the queen, very slowly, "is your name ... John?"

"No!" he laughed. "That is *not* my name!"

"I wonder ..." she said, "could it be ... Tom?"

"No! no!" he laughed. "That is *not* my name!"

"Well ..." said the queen, "is it ...

RUMPELSTILTSKIN?"

"Who told you?" he shouted. "Who? Who?"

The little man was so angry. He stamped and stamped until he had stamped a hole in the floor, and then he whooshed right through it. And that was that. He was never seen again!

Then the queen picked up her baby, and she gave her lovely baby a great, big gorgeous hug!

Snow White and the Seven Dwarfs

Once upon a time there was a princess and her name was Snow White. She was a very pretty princess. She had shiny black hair, lips that were red as cherries, and skin that was white as snow.

When Snow White was quite small, her mother died and her father, the king, married again. The new queen was beautiful. But she was also proud and very vain.

She had a magic mirror, and when she looked

in it, she said:

"Mirror, mirror on the wall,
Who is the loveliest one of all?"

And the mirror always answered:

"You are the loveliest, O Queen!"

But Snow White was growing prettier and prettier, and one day when the queen looked in the mirror and asked her usual question, the mirror answered:

"O Queen, you are lovely, it is true,
But Snow White is lovelier far than you!"

"Then Snow White shall die!" said the queen. And she ordered one of her huntsmen to take Snow White into the forest and kill her.

But the huntsman could not bear to hurt the lovely young girl, so he took her into the forest and left her there, all alone. Poor Snow White wandered through the forest, and at last she came to a little cottage. She knocked at the door, but no one answered, so she turned the handle and walked in.

Everything inside was bright and clean and tidy. The table was laid with seven little knives, seven little forks, seven little loaves on seven little plates and seven little glasses of wine. Around the table were seven little chairs and along one wall were seven little beds.

Snow White was tired and hungry, so she ate some bread from each plate and drank some wine from each glass. Then she lay down on one of the beds and fell asleep.

When it was almost dark, the door opened and in came seven dwarfs. They lit seven little candles, and at once they knew that things were not exactly the same as when they had left home. They said:

"Who's been sitting on my chair?"

"Who's been eating my bread?"

"Who's been drinking my wine?"

"Who moved my plate?"

"Who's been cutting with my knife?"

"Who touched my fork?"

Then the seventh dwarf said, "And who's that, lying on my bed?"

They lifted their candles and the light fell on Snow White. "Oh!" they said. "What a lovely girl!"

Snow White woke, and when she saw seven dwarfs looking down at her, she *was* surprised. But the dwarfs were so friendly that she soon told

them all about herself.

"Stay with us, Snow White," they said. "But be careful. When we go to work, keep the door locked. Don't let anyone in and don't take anything from anybody, because the wicked queen may still try to harm you."

From then on Snow White lived with the seven dwarfs. Every day she cleaned the cottage and cooked for them, while they went to work in the hills where they dug for gold.

But one day, back at the palace, the queen looked in the mirror and asked her usual question, and the mirror answered:

"O Queen, you are lovely, it is true,
But Snow White is lovelier far than you!
And in the hills, in the forest shade,
With seven dwarfs her home she has made!"

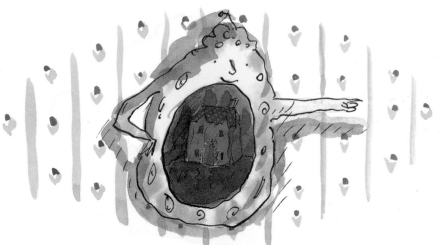

"Then Snow White shall die!" said the wicked queen. "But this time I will see to it myself!"

First she found out where the seven dwarfs lived. Then she filled a basket with some beautiful ripe apples and put some poison on the biggest apple. She only put the poison on the rosy-red side – she didn't touch the green side. Then the wicked queen disguised herself as a poor old woman and, with the basket of apples on her arm, off she went.

When she came to the seven dwarfs' cottage, she knocked at the door and called out, "Ripe apples for sale!"

Snow White opened the window. "I am very sorry," she said, "but I must not buy anything from anybody!"

The old woman quietly picked up the biggest apple. She cut it in half and began to eat the green

half. Then she held out the rosy-red half – which was poisoned – and she said, "Here is a piece of my sweet, juicy apple! Just for you!"

And the old woman seemed so kind, and the apple looked so delicious, that Snow White reached out her hand and took it. She bit into the apple … and then she fell to the floor as if she were dead.

The wicked queen hurried back to the palace. She looked in the mirror and asked her usual question, and the mirror answered:

"*You are the loveliest, O Queen!*"

"Good!" said the wicked queen.

When the seven dwarfs came home and found Snow White lying on the floor, they tried to wake her, but they could not.

They were very sad, and they could not bear to bury their lovely Snow White in the cold ground. So they made a glass coffin for her and wrote in gold letters on the lid:

SNOW WHITE – A ROYAL PRINCESS

Then they placed the glass coffin high on a hillside, and took turns to sit beside it and watch over her.

For a long time Snow White lay in the coffin – and still she was as beautiful as ever. Her hair

was shiny black, her lips were red as cherries and her skin was white as snow.

One day a prince came riding by, and when he saw Snow White, he fell in love with her, and asked the dwarfs if he could take the glass coffin back to his father's palace.

Although the dwarfs did not want to lose Snow White, they could see that the prince loved her, so they agreed. But as they lifted the coffin, one of the dwarfs stumbled and jolted it … and the piece of poisoned apple fell out of Snow

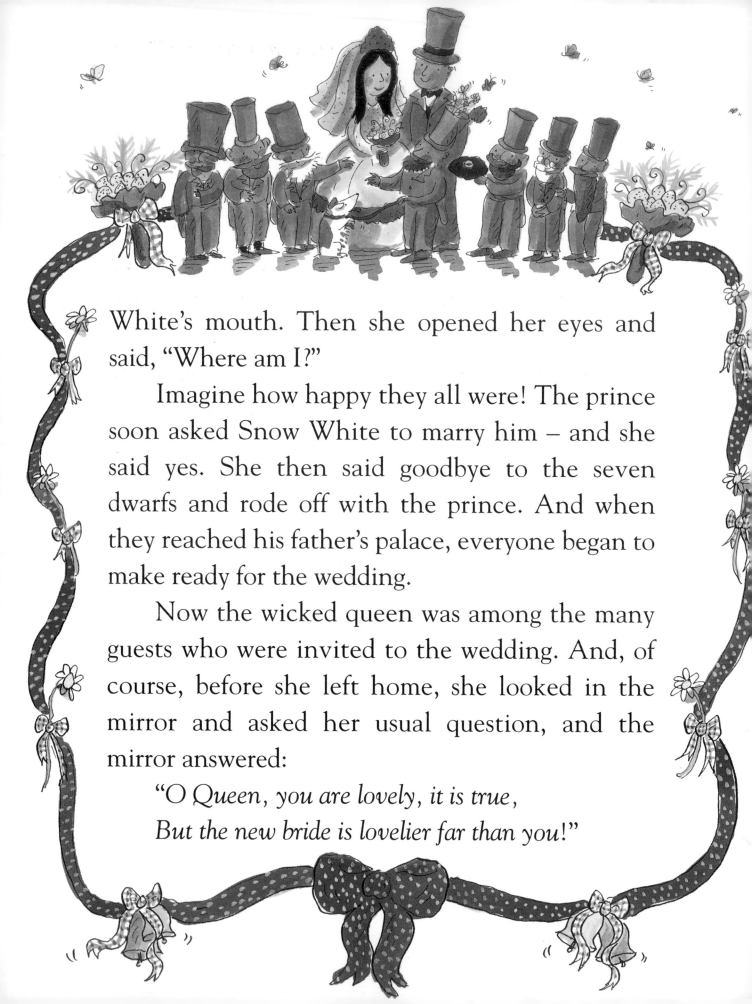

White's mouth. Then she opened her eyes and said, "Where am I?"

Imagine how happy they all were! The prince soon asked Snow White to marry him – and she said yes. She then said goodbye to the seven dwarfs and rode off with the prince. And when they reached his father's palace, everyone began to make ready for the wedding.

Now the wicked queen was among the many guests who were invited to the wedding. And, of course, before she left home, she looked in the mirror and asked her usual question, and the mirror answered:

"*O Queen, you are lovely, it is true,*
But the new bride is lovelier far than you!"

"I must see this new bride!" said the queen, and she hurried off to the wedding.

When she got there and saw that the beautiful bride was Snow White, the wicked queen was overcome by such a furious rage that, there and then, she fell to the floor and died.

But Snow White and the prince and the seven dwarfs, they all lived happily ever after!

The Frog Prince

There was once a little princess who had seven sisters. But they were all older than her and quite grown up, so every day she had to play in the palace gardens by herself.

One day she was playing with her favourite toy – a lovely golden ball that sparkled when she tossed it in the air – and the ball fell SPLASH! into the lily pond. The little princess was upset,

and she began to cry.

Then she heard a strange, croaky voice say, "I will find your ball. But you must give me something in return!"

She looked around and saw a frog, sitting on a waterlily leaf. "Frog," she said, "I'll give you anything you want if you fetch my ball! My necklace, my bracelet … anything!"

"I do not want your necklace or your bracelet," said the frog. "I only want you to promise to be my friend and let me eat from your plate and sleep on your soft bed."

The princess didn't like frogs. She didn't like their bulgy eyes and their cold, damp skin. But she thought, "He's only a silly frog, and I won't ever see him again." So she said, "I promise."

Then the frog dived into the pond, and a few minutes later he came swimming back with the golden ball and threw it on the grass.

The little princess picked it up. "Thank you, frog," she said. And then she turned round and ran off!

"Wait for me!" called the frog. "I can't run fast like you. I can only jump."

But the little princess ran even faster.

That evening the king, the queen, the seven grown-up sisters and the little princess were sitting in the dining room, eating their supper, when they heard a strange noise. *Ker-plump! ker-plump! ker-*

plump! Something was coming up the marble staircase.

There was a knock at the door, and a croaky voice called out, "Little princess! Open the door and let me in!"

The king stopped eating, the queen stopped eating, the seven grown-up sisters stopped eating – and they all looked at the little princess. She jumped up, ran to the door and opened it. And there was THE FROG!

As soon as she saw him, she banged the door shut, ran back to the table and sat down.

"Who was that knocking at the door?" asked

her father, the king.

"It was a frog," she said.

"And what does Mr Croaky Water-splasher want from you?" he asked.

Then she told the king all about her golden ball and the promise she had made.

"My little princess," said her father, "you must always keep a promise. Now open the door and let him in."

So she walked slowly to the door and opened it, and the frog came jumping into the room.

When he reached the table, he said, "Please lift me up."

"Ugh!" said the little princess. She didn't want to touch the frog.

"Remember your promise," said her father. So she lifted the frog, with one finger and one thumb, and dropped him on the table.

"I can't reach your plate," said the frog. So she pushed her plate close to the frog, and he began to eat.

"Ugh!" she said. She was not going to eat from the same plate as a *frog*!

When the frog had finished eating, he said, "Little princess, please carry me up to your bed."

"No, I won't!" she said. "I don't want to carry you!"

"Remember your promise," said her father. So the princess lifted the frog, with one finger and one thumb, and carried him up to her bedroom. Then she dropped him on the floor, in the corner furthest away from her bed.

"Remember your promise," said the frog. "You must let me sleep on your bed." So she lifted the frog, with one finger and one thumb, and dropped

him on the bed, right at the bottom.

"Please," said the frog. "I would like to sleep on your pillow."

"No!" she answered. "I didn't promise that. You must stay at the bottom of the bed." Then she climbed into bed and fell asleep.

The next morning when she woke, the first thing she saw was THE FROG. He was sitting on her pillow, staring at her with his big bulgy eyes.

"Ugh!" she said and grabbed hold of him and threw him off the bed. And the frog hit the wall, fell to the floor and lay there, quiet and still.

The little princess was upset. She hadn't meant to hurt the frog. She climbed out of bed, picked him up and stroked him. "Poor frog, please don't die," she said.

Then she kissed him … and the frog was gone … and there was a prince. A very handsome prince!

He said, "Thank you, little princess! You have set me free from a wicked witch's evil spell."

And he told her his story. How one day when he was riding through a forest, a witch had caught

him and changed him into a frog. And how only a kiss from a princess could change him back into a prince again.

Well, after that, the little princess and the frog prince really did become good friends. And when she grew older, they married and lived happily ever after!

Hansel and Gretel

Once upon a time a boy and girl called Hansel and Gretel lived with their father and stepmother, in a little house beside a big forest. The family was very poor. There was never enough to eat and they were always hungry.

One night when the children were in bed, their stepmother said to their father, "We must take Hansel and Gretel into the forest and leave

them there because we can't feed them any more."

"Oh, no! I won't do that!" said their father. "I love my children!"

"But we must," said their stepmother. "We have no money, and there's not enough food in the house to feed us all."

Now Hansel and Gretel were so hungry, they couldn't sleep, and they heard what their stepmother said.

Gretel began to cry. But Hansel whispered, "Don't cry, little sister. I'll look after you!" And he rolled out of bed, put on his jacket, crept into the garden and filled his pockets with some white pebbles that were shining, all silvery, in the moonlight.

In the morning the children's stepmother gave them a piece of dry bread to eat and told them to hurry, because the whole family was going into the forest to collect firewood. Then off they went together. But Hansel walked behind the others and, every now and then, he dropped a

white pebble on the path.

After a while, they came to a clearing in the forest. Then the children's stepmother said, "Wait here, while we go a little further and chop down some trees."

So Hansel and Gretel sat down. But they were tired and soon fell asleep, and when they woke, it was night and the moon was in the sky.

Hansel looked around, and he found his pebbles shining, all silvery, in the moonlight. So he took Gretel by the hand, they followed the trail

of pebbles, and it led them back to their own little house.

Their father was very happy when he saw them, but their stepmother was not. The next night she said to their father, "We must take Hansel and Gretel into the forest again, and this time we must make sure they don't come back!"

Once again, the children were awake, and when they heard what was said, Hansel crept off to collect some more pebbles. But the door was locked and the key was gone, so he could not go outside.

In the morning their stepmother gave them a piece of dry bread to eat. But Hansel put it in his pocket. Then the family went off into the forest to collect more firewood. But Hansel walked behind the others and, every now and then, he dropped a small white breadcrumb on the path.

When they had gone a long way into the forest, their stepmother said to the children, "Wait here, while we go and chop down some trees."

Once again, Hansel and Gretel sat down and fell asleep. When they woke, it was night and the moon was in the sky. Hansel looked around, but he could not see the breadcrumbs he had dropped. The birds of the forest had flown down and eaten every single one!

Now Hansel did not know which way to go, but he took Gretel by the hand, and they walked and walked. All through the night they walked. Morning came, and they walked on.

At last they came to a clearing in the forest … and there was a house, a strange and wonderful house! It had gingerbread walls, barley-sugar windows and a chocolate door, while the roof was made of cakes and cookies, decorated with twists and twirls of icing.

Hansel snapped off a lump of icing and bit into it. Gretel broke off a piece of gingerbread and popped it in her mouth.

And then, all of a sudden, the door opened, and an old woman with ruby-red eyes came out.

She said, "Who's that nibbling at my house?"

"I'm sorry," said Hansel, "but we're very hungry."

"Then come in," said the old woman, "and I shall give you some supper."

So Hansel and Gretel went into the house, and the old woman gave them each a glass of milk, some pancakes and an apple. When they had

eaten the food, she took them into a room where there were two little beds. And it was not long before Hansel and Gretel were curled up in those beds, fast asleep.

They did not know that the old woman was a WITCH, who caught children who were lost in the forest and ate them!

In the morning the witch crept in, bent down over the sleeping children and looked at them very closely. She had to do that, because she could not see clearly with her ruby-red eyes.

"They are too thin to eat!" she said. "Much too thin!"

She shook Hansel and woke him... and she took him and put him in a cage. She shook Gretel and shouted, "Get up, lazy-bones! Light the fire! Wash the dishes! Scrub the floor! And be quick about it!"

From that time on, Gretel had to work very hard. But Hansel was kept in the cage. The witch gave him lots of food to make him fat, and every

day she said to him, "Show me your finger so I can see how fat you are."

Now Hansel had found a small chicken bone in the cage and ... *guess what he did.* He pushed out the bone instead of his finger!

When the witch felt the bone, she always said, "Still too thin! Much too thin!"

But after a while, the witch grew tired of waiting for Hansel to grow fat, and one morning she said to Gretel, "Light the fire and heat the

oven, because today – fat or thin – I am going to roast your brother and eat him!"

So Gretel lit the fire. When the oven was very hot, the witch said, "Climb into the oven and see if it is hot enough."

But Gretel was a sensible girl and she was not going to climb into a hot oven. She said, "You must show me how to do it."

"Open the door like this," said the witch, and she opened the door. "Put in your head like this." And she leant forward.

Then Gretel gave her a hard push, and the witch went head over heels into the oven. Gretel slammed the door shut, and that was the end of the wicked witch.

Gretel ran to the cage. She unlocked it, and Hansel was free! Then they opened the witch's treasure chest and filled their pockets with gold and silver and precious jewels.

"Now we must go home," said Hansel. So off they went. They walked and walked and *walked* and at last they came to a path which they knew. They walked faster, and they saw their own little house. And then they ran!

Their father was very happy to see his children. He had missed them and spent every day looking for them in the forest. This had made their stepmother angry and one day she had packed her clothes in a bundle and left. And she did not come back.

From that time on Hansel and Gretel and their father lived happily in their little house beside the big forest. Because of the witch's treasure, they had enough money to buy all the food they needed. So Hansel and Gretel never again went to bed feeling hungry!

The Princess and the Pea

There was once a prince, and he wanted to marry a princess. But she had to be a real princess. So he went to look for one.

He travelled to lots of countries and met lots of princesses, but there was always something the matter with them. Some were too grumpy, some were too ugly, some were too proud and some were very boring and dull. And then some were not *real* princesses. They were only pretending.

At last the prince came home, and he said to his father, the king, and his mother, the queen, "I am disappointed. I have looked everywhere, and I cannot find a real princess to marry."

One night there was a great storm. Thunder boomed, lightning flashed and rain came pouring down. In the middle of the storm, there was a knock at the castle door, and the king went and opened it. Standing on the doorstep was a young girl. Her hair was dripping wet, her clothes were soaked and she was shivering with the cold.

"Who are you?" asked the king.

"I am a princess," said the girl.

The king thought, "She doesn't look like a princess to me." But all the same, he invited her in and took her to meet the queen and the prince.

"This girl was standing at the door," said the king. "She *says* she is a princess."

Then the girl gave such a merry smile that the prince thought, "If she is a real princess, I shall marry her!"

The queen thought, "She does not look like a princess to me. But I'll soon find out about that!" And she hurried off to the guest bedroom.

First the queen took everything off the bed.

Then she put one very small dry pea on the bedstead. She piled twenty mattresses on top of the pea and twenty feather quilts on top of the mattresses. Then she arranged the pillows and bedclothes. And right on top of all those quilts and mattresses was where the girl had to sleep that night.

At breakfast the next morning, the queen said to the girl, "Did you sleep well?"

"No," said the girl. "I didn't sleep a wink. I was so uncomfortable. There was a hard little lump in my bed. And now I am covered in bruises!"

"Ah! Then you must be a *real* princess," said the queen. "Only a *real* princess could feel a pea through twenty mattresses and twenty quilts. Nobody else has such delicate skin."

dry Pea

95

The king nodded his head. He agreed.

And the prince said, "I think you are the sort of princess I have been looking for!"

So, in the end, the prince married the princess who came knocking at the castle door, one wet stormy night!

And what happened to the pea? The prince put it in a special case, in a special museum, so that everyone could come and admire that very special dry pea!